Ben and the Scaredy-Dog

Written by Sarah Ellis   Illustrated by Kim LaFave

pajamapress

First published in Canada and the United States in 2018

This is a first edition.

10 9 8 7 6 5 4 3 2 1

www.pajamapress.ca info@pajamapress.ca

The publisher gratefully acknowledges the support of the Canada Council for the Arts and the Ontario Arts Council for its publishing program. We acknowledge the financial support of the Government of Canada through the Canada Book Fund (CBF) for our publishing activities.

Library and Archives Canada Cataloguing in Publication

Ellis, Sarah, author
Ben and the scaredy-dog / written by Sarah Ellis; illustrated by Kim La Fave.
ISBN 978-1-77278-044-4 (hardcover)
I. LaFave, Kim, illustrator II. Title.
PS8559.L57B47 2018 jC813'.54
C2017-905604-2

Publisher Cataloging-in-Publication Data (U.S.)

Names: Ellis, Sarah, 1952-, author. | LaFave, Kim, illustrator.
Title: Ben and the Scaredy-Dog / written by Sarah Ellis ; illustrated by Kim LaFave.
Description: Toronto, Ontario, Canada : Pajama Press, 2018. | Summary: "Ben is excited to make friends with the new kid across the street, until he learns that Erv has a dog. Ben is afraid of dogs. When it turns out the new dog is afraid of things too, Ben discovers his own unexpected bravery and makes a new kind of friend"— Provided by publisher.
Identifiers: ISBN 978-1-77278-044-4 (hardcover)
Subjects: LCSH: Fear in children – Juvenile fiction. | Dogs – Juvenile fiction. | Fear in animals – Juvenile fiction. | BISAC: JUVENILE FICTION / Animals / Dogs. | JUVENILE FICTION / Social Themes / New Experience.
Classification: LCC PZ7.E455Ben |DDC [E] – dc23

Original art created digitally
Cover and book design—Rebecca Bender

Manufactured by QuaLibre Inc./PrintPlus
Printed in China

Pajama Press Inc.
181 Carlaw Ave. Suite 207 Toronto, Ontario Canada, M4M 2S1

Distributed in Canada by UTP Distribution
5201 Dufferin Street Toronto, Ontario Canada, M3H 5T8

Distributed in the U.S. by Ingram Publisher Services
1 Ingram Blvd. La Vergne, TN 37086, USA

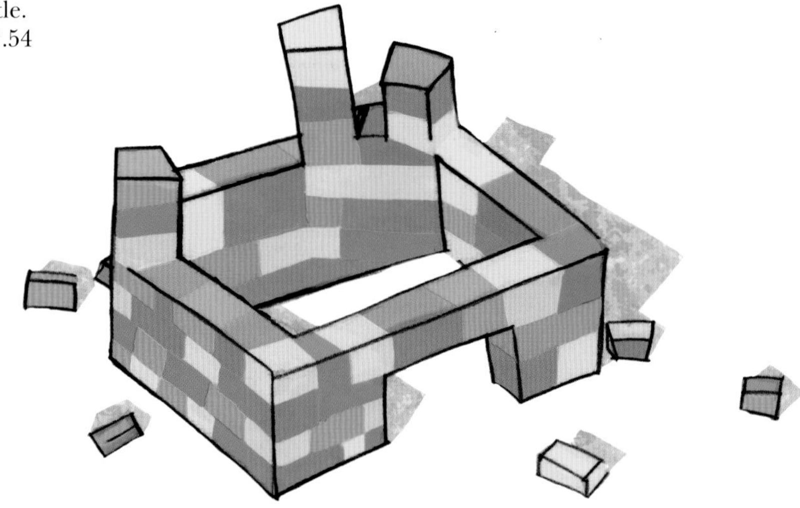

For Judi and Libbie and Sally-Dog
—S.E.

For Jeff and Miwa
—K. La F.

What do you see when you look at a dog?

Ben's big sister Robin sees fun, fetch, floppy ears, sit, stay, and tug-of-war.

Ben's big brother Joe sees wagging tails, licking tongues, and love, love, love.

When Ben looks at a dog he sees jaws and teeth. That's a dog to Ben. Jaws and teeth.

Ben watched a new family move in across the street. Beds and boxes, chests and chairs, rugs in rolls. And, **finally**, a kid. A kid his age. Maybe a friend? Ben thought he would go over and say hello.

But **finally** wasn't a kid. **Finally** was a dog. A big dog. Big jaws. Big teeth.

Ben changed his mind about visiting the new kid.

The new kid, named Erv, came to Ben's house the next day with her mom and her dog. The dog's name was Max. They all sat in Ben's backyard.

Ben liked Erv right away. Erv was short for Minerva, like Ben was short for Benjamin. She could whistle, snap her fingers, blow a double bubble, and do a perfect cartwheel.

Ben didn't like Max. Max left dog-slobber on Ben's hand, and he gave a big, loud bark when he spotted Ben's cat. But at least Erv kept him on a leash.

"You must come over to our place when we've unpacked," said Erv's mom.

Ben hoped the unpacking would take a long time.

It didn't. The next weekend, Erv invited Ben over to play with her Lotsablox.

Ben didn't want to go. He told Robin.

"It's the dog, right?" said Robin.

"He won't be on a leash in his own house," said Ben.

“You can do it,” said Robin. “Think positive. Just say to yourself, ‘Big Brave Ben, Big Brave Ben.’ Give it a try.”

Ben didn’t think positive, but he did decide to give it a try.

The playroom was mostly empty, except for a bath mat with Max on it.

“Why’s he sitting there?”

“It’s the shiny floor. We didn’t have shiny floors in our old house and Max is scared of them. We don’t know why. We’re trying to get him used to it.”

Erv kissed Max on the nose and used that dog-talking voice that dog people use. “You’re just an old scaredy-dog aren’t you, Maxi?”

There was lots of space in the shiny-floor room to build the ruins of a dragon palace. It took all afternoon and all the Lotsablox.

Ben almost forgot about the dog.

But then Erv's mom called her.
"Grandma's online. Come talk to her."

That left Ben alone in the room with Max, a dog between him and the door.

Ben went over everything he had heard about dogs.

Dogs can smell your fear. Ben tried not to be smelly.

Don't look a dog in the eye. Ben squinched his eyes shut in case he looked at Max by mistake.

He talked positive to himself. “He won’t get off the mat. He won’t get off the mat.”

Then he heard a sound.

— Tickety-tick

It was the sound of dog toenails on a shiny floor.

What could he do? There was no escape. Could he protect himself with the ruins of the dragon palace?

Could he make a dash for it? No. *If you run, dogs chase you and knock you down and bite you with their strong jaws and big, sharp teeth.*

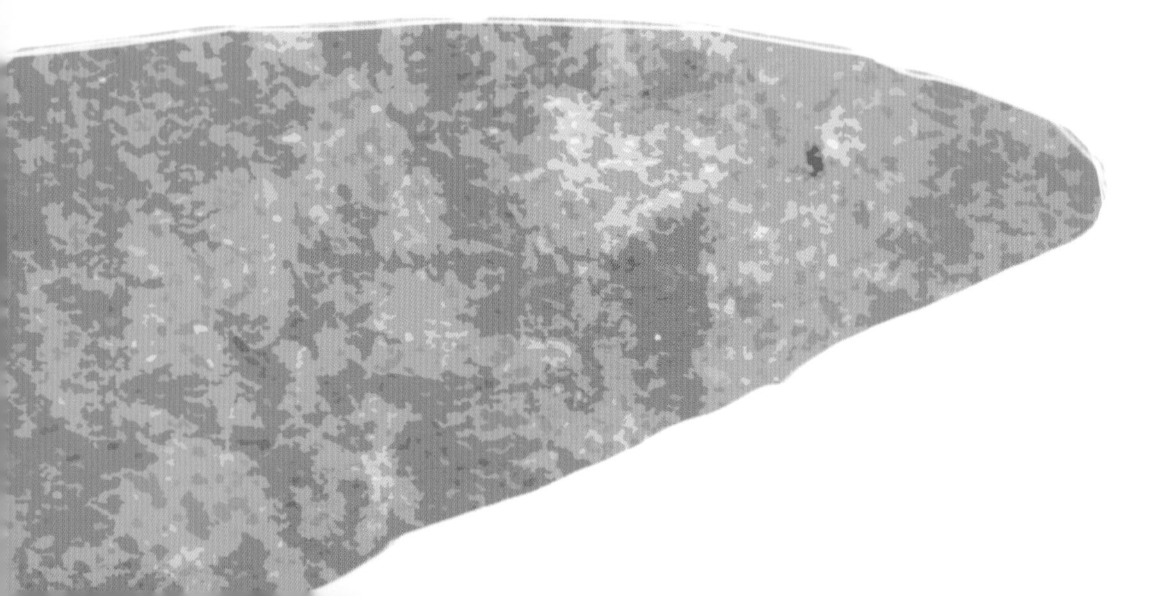

Ben started humming. The only tune he could think of was “Happy Birthday.”

Tickety-
tick

Ben hummed louder.

Tickety-tick

Tickety-tick

Tickety-
tick

Ben hummed louder still. He hum-sang for all he was worth.

"Happy birthday, Big Brave Ben.
Happy birthday to you."

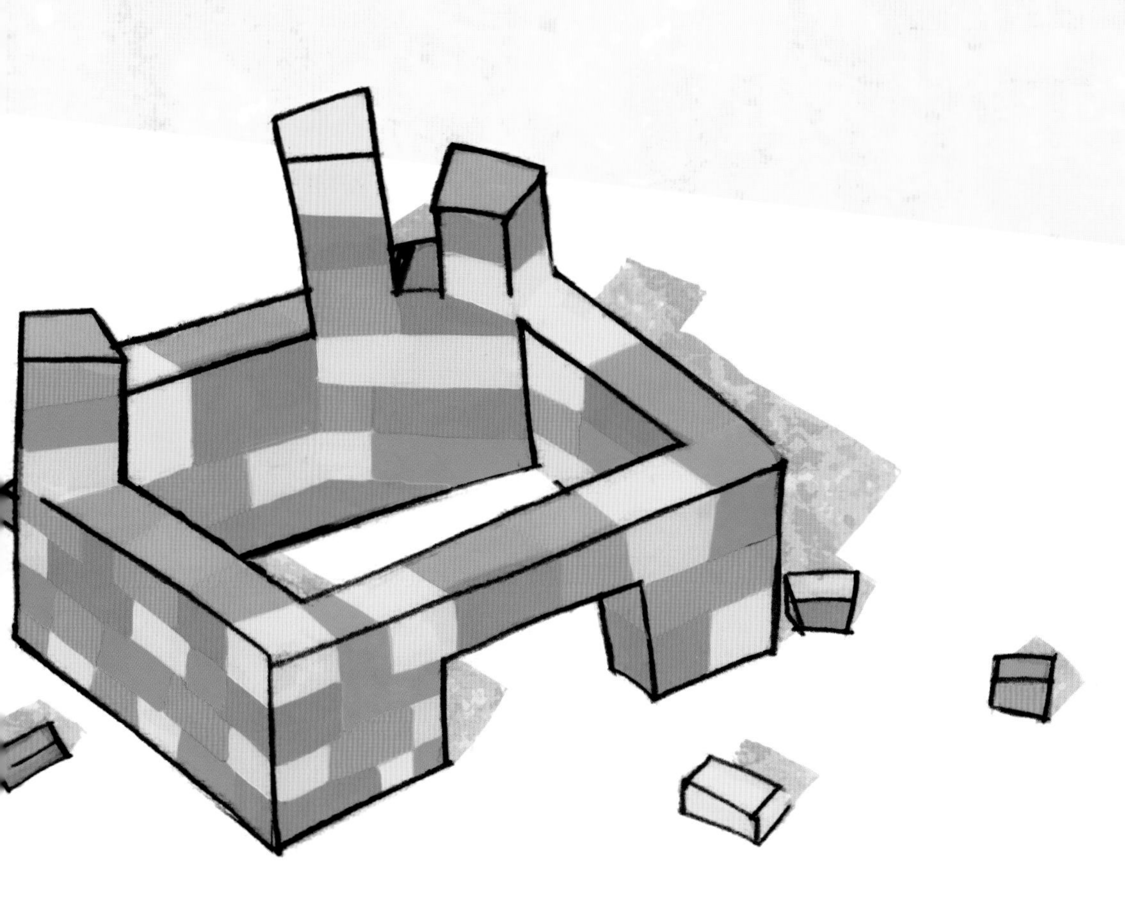

The ticking stopped and Ben felt something lean against him. Something warm and heavy.

No barking, no biting, no licking, no butting, no jumping, no sniffing. Just leaning.

Ben took a big breath. Max took a big breath. Ben leaned in. Max leaned in. There was no sound at all.

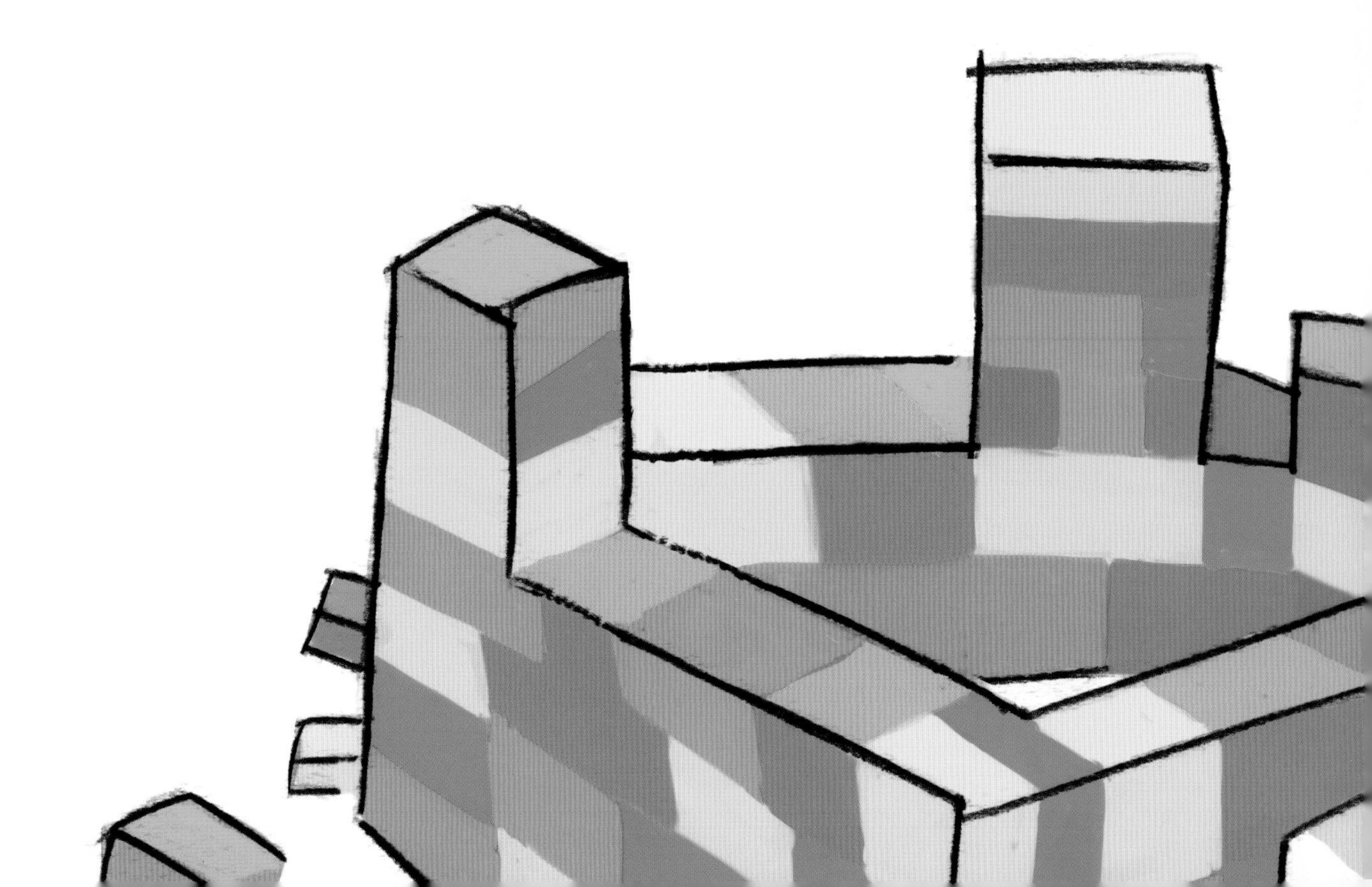

Erv and her mom came bursting into the room.

“Hey! Look at Max! How did you get him to cross the shiny floor?”

“I hummed,” said Ben.

Erv wrapped her arms around Max. She talked in her dog-talking voice. “What a good boy! What a brave dog.”

Ben let himself look. He didn't see jaws and teeth. He saw a brave, friendly leaner. Max hardly seemed like a dog at all.

"It's amazing," said Erv's mom. "You must have a way with dogs."

A way with dogs? thought Ben. Well, maybe a way with one scaredy-dog. Big Brave Ben gave Max a little pat on his big head.

Max wagged his tail.

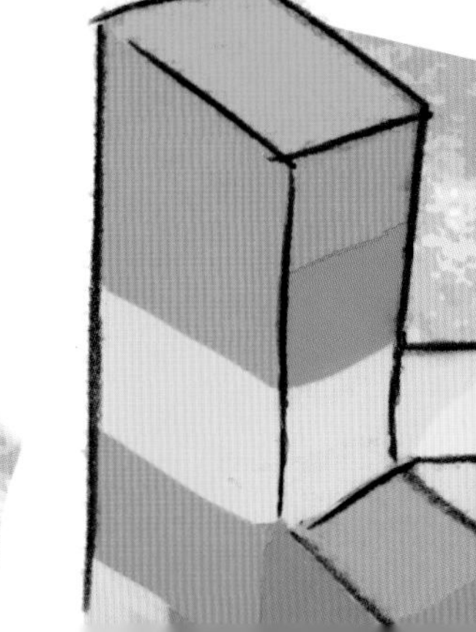